PROFILES

Nelson Mandela

Mary Benson

Illustrated by
Karen Heywood

Hamish Hamilton
London

Titles in the Profiles *series*

Muhammad Ali	0-241-10600-1	John Lennon	0-241-11561-2
Chris Bonington	0-241-11044-0	Martin Luther King	0-241-10931-0
Ian Botham	0-241-11031-9	Nelson Mandela	0-241-11913-8
Geoffrey Boycott	0-241-10712-1	Bob Marley	0-241-11476-4
Edith Cavell	0-241-11479-9	Paul McCartney	0-241-10930-2
Charlie Chaplin	0-241-10479-3	Montgomery of Alamein	0-241-11562-0
Winston Churchill	0-241-10482-3	Lord Mountbatten	0-241-10593-5
Sebastian Coe	0-241-10848-9	Florence Nightingale	0-241-11477-2
Marie Curie	0-241-11741-0	Rudolf Nureyev	0-241-10849-7
Roald Dahl	0-241-11043-2	Emmeline Pankhurst	0-241-11478-0
Thomas Edison	0-241-10713-X	Pope John Paul II	0-241-10711-3
Queen Elizabeth II	0-241-10850-0	Anna Pavlova	0-241-10481-5
The Queen Mother	0-241-11030-0	Prince Philip	0-241-11167-6
Alexander Fleming	0-241-11203-6	Lucinda Prior-Palmer	0-241-10710-5
Anne Frank	0-241-11294-X	Barry Sheene	0-241-10851-9
Indira Gandhi	0-241-11772-0	Mother Teresa	0-241-10933-7
Gandhi	0-241-11166-8	Margaret Thatcher	0-241-10596-X
Basil Hume	0-241-11204-4	Daley Thompson	0-241-10932-9
Kevin Keegan	0-241-10594-3	Queen Victoria	0-241-10480-7
Helen Keller	0-241-11295-8	The Princess of Wales	0-241-11740-2

First published 1986 by
Hamish Hamilton Children's Books
27 Wrights Lane, London W8 5TZ

British Library Cataloguing in Publication Data
Benson, Mary
Nelson Mandela.—(Profiles)
1. Mandela, Nelson—Juvenile literature
2. Political prisoners—South Africa—
Biography—Juvenile literature 3. South
Africa—Race relations—Juvenile
literature 4. South Africa—Politics and
government—20th century—Juvenile
literature
I. Title II. Series
322.4'4'0924 DT779.95.M36
ISBN 0-241-11913-8
Typeset by Pioneer, Perthshire
Printed in Great Britain at the
University Press, Cambridge

Contents

1	A DESIRE TO SERVE THE PEOPLE	9
2	UP AGAINST THE 'INSANE POLICY' OF APARTHEID	13
3	OPEN THE JAIL DOORS! WE WANT TO ENTER!	18
4	TREATED AS A CRIMINAL	22
5	COULD THIS BE HIGH TREASON?	25
6	HOW MANY BRIDESMAIDS DO YOU WANT?	30
7	THE BLACK PIMPERNEL	34
8	'I WILL STILL BE MOVED. . . .'	39
9	'RIVONIA IS A NAME TO REMEMBER'	42
10	MANDELA TAUGHT ME HOW TO SURVIVE	47
11	'RELEASE MANDELA!'	54

Nelson Mandela

1 A Desire to Serve The People

When a son was born to Chief Henry Gadla Mandela and his wife, Nonqaphi, on 18 July 1918, they gave him the Xhosa name of Rolihlahla and, because it was the fashion to have a European name, preferably a heroic one, they also called him Nelson.

The boy and his three sisters lived in the family kraal of whitewashed huts not far from Umtata in the Transkei. Although the Mandelas were members of the royal family of the Thembu people, Nelson, like most African children, herded sheep and cattle and helped with the ploughing.

As a young boy he was tall for his age, and was a fast runner. He hunted buck and, when hungry, stole mealie cobs from the maize fields. He loved the countryside with its grassy rolling hills, and the stream which flowed eastward to the Indian ocean.

At night, under Africa's brilliant stars, everyone used to gather around a big open fire to listen to the elders of the tribe. The boy was fascinated by the tales told by these bearded old men. Tales about the 'good old days before the coming of the white man', and tales about the brave acts performed by their ancestors, in defending their country against the European invaders.

Those tales, said Mandela many years later when he was on trial for his life, stirred in him a desire to serve his people in their struggle to be free. A desire which eventually led to his becoming the most famous political prisoner of our time – a prisoner with songs written about him and streets named after him. How appropriate that Nelson Mandela's Xhosa name, Rolihlahla, means 'stirring up trouble'.

When Nelson first went to school – a school for African children – it was a shock to find the history books described only white heroes, and referred to his people as savages and cattle thieves. All the same he was eager for 'western' education, and proud that his great-grandfather had given land on which to build a mission school. Even when fellow-pupils teased him about his clothes, cast-offs from his father, he pretended not to mind.

At home he picked up information not taught at school, about how Dutch and British settlers with guns had fought and defeated blacks with spears, and taken almost all of their land. Then, how the British, after defeating the Dutch in the Boer War (Boer was the Dutch word for farmer), had shared power with their former enemy. Despite passionate protests from Africans and liberal whites, the British government gave the million white South Africans total control over the 4½ million 'non-whites' – Africans, Asians and those of mixed race, known as 'Coloured' people. The Boers, calling themselves Afrikaners, had become an important part of the all-white parliament which passed more and more colour bar laws. They aimed at keeping

The family kraal

Africans — 'natives' — as labourers and servants, who were not allowed to move freely in their own country and were forced to live in 'reserves' or 'locations'. Such inhuman policies could only be maintained by force and, from earliest childhood, Nelson heard names such as Bulhoek and Bondelswarts — names which recalled the massacre of hundreds of Africans.

In 1930 Henry Mandela fell seriously ill. Realising that he was dying, he presented his son to the Paramount Chief. He asked that the boy be given a good education. So Nelson became the ward of David Dalindyebo, and lived in a modest hut at the Chief's Great Place, Mqekezweni. Fitted with new clothes, he went to a Methodist boarding school.

Soon it was time for the traditional rite of circumcision and, aged sixteen, he spent several weeks in the mountains with others of his age group. The tribal elders led them through ceremonies, preparing them for manhood.

He continued to respect his people's customs even as he went on to study for a Bachelor of Arts degree at Fort Hare – a college for Africans in the Eastern Cape. Although he was not clever, he worked hard and was very popular. However, his studies were cut short when he was suspended for taking part in a students' strike. Returning home, he was ordered by the Paramount Chief to give up the protest. He might have obeyed but for an unexpected development. 'My guardian,' he later explained, 'felt it was time for me to get married. He loved me very much, but he was no democrat and did not think it worthwhile to consult me about a wife. He selected a girl, fat and dignified, and arrangements were made for the wedding.'

By this time, Nelson had also realized that he was being groomed for chieftainship, and had no wish to rule over an oppressed people. He decided to run away.

2 Up Against The 'Insane Policy' of Apartheid

Mandela, a handsome, very tall and athletic twenty-two year old, set off for Johannesburg by train. The carriage was labelled for NON-EUROPEANS. He was but one of the many thousands flocking to Egoli, the city of gold, in search of jobs; South Africa supported Britain in the war against Hitler's Nazi Germany and there was a great demand for labour in wartime industries.

He was thrust into a world of large buildings, noisy fast traffic and crowds of all races. He found that in the city, buses and trams, restaurants and cafés, and public toilets, were all reserved for whites. Even the park benches were labelled EUROPEANS ONLY. He saw little of the 'white' suburbs with their spacious gardens as he made his way to one of the teeming 'native' locations.

Without electricity, drainage, tarred roads or telephones, these areas were continually being raided by police, arresting blacks under the hated pass laws. Like all African men Mandela now needed a pass to get a job, to live in a town, to travel and to be out after curfew — 11 p.m. — at night. Without it he could be fined or imprisoned. But he quickly discovered that in

Nelson Mandela aged 19

the midst of poverty and suffering, the people were full of life and found much to laugh at.

He himself had a tremendous sense of humour, and thought his first job quite comic. He had hoped to become a clerk but, on applying at a gold mine, was taken on as a policeman, guarding the gate, armed with knobkerrie (a heavy, knobbed stick) and whistle. However, a representative of the Paramount Chief tracked him down, and he was on the run again.

Someone suggested that he should meet Walter Sisulu, a mature self-educated man who was also from the Transkei. Sisulu befriended Mandela. When Mandela mentioned an ambition to study law, Sisulu helped him financially and introduced him to a firm of white lawyers.

Here Mandela had his first direct experience of 'Europeans', as whites called themselves. Later in life he told of these incidents with much amusement. 'Look, Nelson,' the senior secretary said on his first morning. 'We have no colour bar here. When the teaboy brings the tea, come and get yours from the tray. We have bought two new cups for you and Gaur, the clerk. You *must* use them!'

On another day, he was dictating to a typist when a white client came in; the girl, wanting to show that Mandela was not her superior, took sixpence from her purse. 'Nelson,' she said, 'please go and get me some shampoo from the chemist.'

While still a student, Mandela fell in love with Evelyn Ntoko Mase, a pretty nurse with a soft voice. After they were married, she generously helped to pay for his studies. They set up home in Orlando, a township of matchbox houses about 16 kilometres south-west of Johannesburg, in an area later named Soweto.

Keen on keeping fit, Mandela was becoming an excellent boxer, but he was even more interested in politics, stimulated by all he witnessed every day. Like Sisulu he joined the African National Congress. So did a friend from his days at Fort Hare, Oliver Tambo, a brilliant young man teaching maths at an Anglican school for Africans. The three were to become a remarkable team.

The ANC (African National Congress) had been founded in 1912 by four African lawyers who had qualified in Britain and America. Their object was to unite their people. 'Tribal divisions,' they said, 'cause ignorance and woes.' Years of protest followed against one injustice after another – peaceful demonstrations and deputations to which the white governments replied with increasing repression. With other young men and women, Sisulu, Mandela and Tambo founded a Youth League, and eagerly discussed ways of 'galvanising' the ANC to become more militant in its protests.

They admired the courage of African miners who, in 1946, out of desperation at low wages, went on strike. Police drove them back to work; nine miners were killed. That same year Mandela was also impressed by Indian friends, fellow-law students, when they organized passive resistance to government restrictions on the Asian community. (They were descendants of families brought from India by the British to labour in Natal's sugar plantations. Back in 1907 a young lawyer named Gandhi had started passive resistance in South Africa.)

In spite of the failure of such protests, many hoped that because South Africa had taken part in the war against Nazi racism, there would be less segregation in future. Instead, in 1948, the Afrikaner National Party came to power and began to enforce apartheid (pronounced apart-hate), an evil system of racial segregation. Their pro-Nazi sympathies were played down as they claimed to be a 'bastion of western Christian civilization' against the 'red menace'. They won votes by frightening whites with warnings of the *swart gevaar* – the black danger. They would not talk to African leaders. New laws caused increasing suffering for 'non-whites'. Each individual was classified by race, and each race and tribe was to be set apart from every other. The removal of millions of Africans from so-called 'black spots' began. They were taken to remote, dry areas where they were dumped as part of the reorganization of the country. Mandela said that nowhere, except in Hitler's policy towards the Jews, had such an insane policy existed.

At the ANC's annual conference in December 1951, he and Sisulu proposed countrywide defiance of certain laws and, since they faced a heavily armed state, emphasized that the campaign must be strictly non-violent. The conference roared its approval.

Abroad, the press commented that the ANC was not anti-white, but anti-unjust laws – that they were fighting for human dignity and freedom. Nelson Mandela was elected national volunteer-in-chief. His deputy from the South African Indian Congress was Maulvi Cachalia, whose father had been one of the bravest passive resisters alongside Gandhi.

3 Open The Jail Doors! We Want To Enter!

It takes great courage to resist force non-violently. Mandela pointed this out to the men and women who volunteered for the Defiance Campaign. The police would try to frighten people, but no matter how violent they became, volunteers must not strike back.

He toured the country, addressing meetings, and inspiring and instructing people. Other African and Indian leaders organized meetings in their areas, but there were many problems. For example, there was a lack of funds and of basic equipment such as typewriters and telephones. Walter Sisulu, now Secretary-General of ANC, was only paid £5 a month. Besides, the pass laws made travelling difficult and, as Mandela and Tambo found when they visited small towns, the one available train often arrived at night and there were no taxis or hotels for blacks. After walking miles to whatever location they were visiting, they had to knock on a likely-looking door. They might be welcomed by an enthusiastic stranger or rebuffed by the cautious.

In Durban when Mandela addressed a huge crowd there was a sense that history was about to be made. Indians who signed pledges to defy the government were especially moved by joining Africans in freedom songs. One began *'Thina sizwe, Thina sizwe esinsundu . . .'* – We Africans, We Africans! We cry for our land. They took it, Europeans. They must let our country go . . .

Early on a winter's morning – 26 June 1952 – Mandela delivered a letter to the magistrate in a mining town near Johannesburg, announcing that 52 defiers would enter the African location without permits. Soon after, Sisulu and Nana Sita, a veteran Gandhian, led the defiers as they walked into the location, and were promptly arrested.

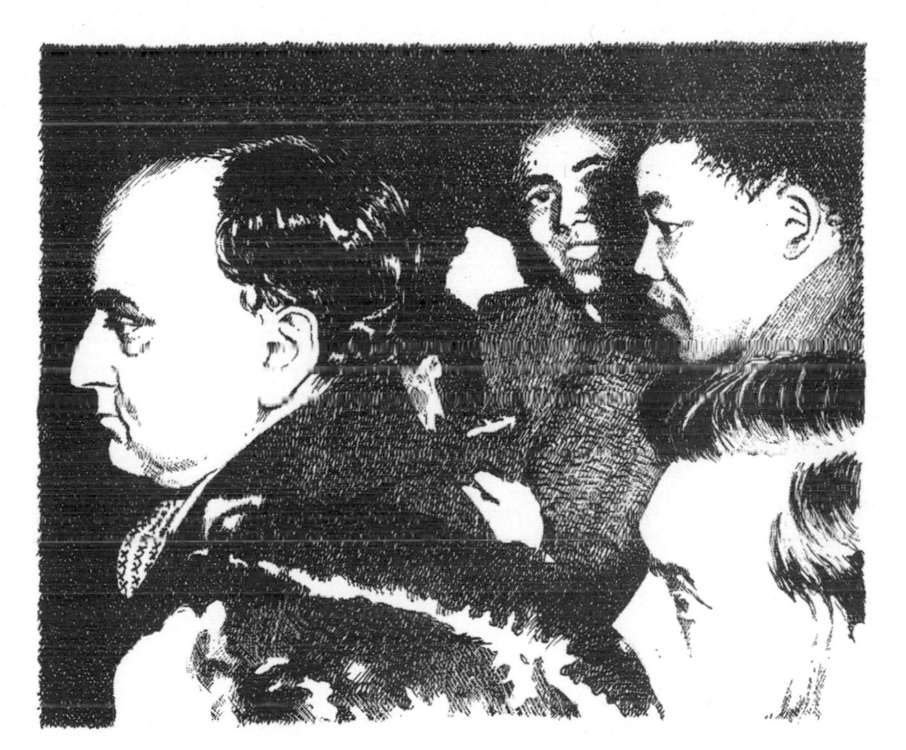

Mandela with supporters in the Defiance Campaign

1,200 kilometres to the south-east, a batch of high-spirited Xhosa women and men set out from New Brighton township in Port Elizabeth, chanting '*Mayibuye Afrika!* – Let Africa return. They marched cheerfully through the EUROPEANS ONLY entrance to the railway station. They were arrested by police and escorted to the other side of the station which, they noted with satisfaction, meant using the EUROPEANS ONLY bridge. A train packed with Africans cheered them. They were singing, 'Open the jail doors, we want to enter, we volunteers . . .'

They were imprisoned for fifteen days.

That night in Johannesburg Mandela addressed a meeting which went on until 11 p.m., the curfew after which Africans needed 'special' passes signed by a European. As they left the hall they were arrested. Singing the ANC anthem, *Nkosi Sikelel' iAfrika* – Lord Bless Africa – they climbed into the police pick-up vans and were driven off.

It was Mandela's first experience of imprisonment. In the police station a white constable pushed one of the defiers, Samuel Makae, so violently that he fell down some steps and broke his ankle. 'I protested,' said Mandela afterwards, 'whereupon the young warrior kicked me on the leg in true cowboy style. We were all indignant and I started a demonstration.' But Mandela's demand that the injured man be given medical attention was curtly refused, and Makae had to spend a frightful night, reeling with pain. Only next morning was he taken to hospital.

During the next four months more than 8,500

volunteers went to jail. Among them were a few whites. None of the laws were repealed. Indeed, the government went on extending apartheid, but many thousands of Africans were politically educated, and ANC membership soared from 7,000 to 100,000.

Mandela was among 'leaders' brought to trial under the Suppression of Communism Act – a law which lumped African protesters together with South Africa's 2,000 communists. Although the judge found them guilty, he pointed out that the law had nothing to do with communism as it is commonly known, and he accepted that the leaders had advised their followers to avoid violence in any shape or form. They were sentenced to nine months' imprisonment, a sentence suspended on condition they did not repeat the offence. The government quickly passed a new law which meant that in future, leaders organizing such protests would be jailed for up to five years or fined up to £500, with a whipping of ten strokes.

4 Treated As A Criminal

Mandela was elected President of the Transvaal ANC. He was not ambitious to lead, his friend Tambo observed. But he was a born mass leader who could not help magnetizing people.

Before he could take over, the security police delivered orders which banned him from gatherings and forbade him to leave Johannesburg. The bans stated that the Minister of Justice considered Mandela guilty of furthering the aims of communism. No reasons were given, no proof was required, no appeal allowed. Soon a further ban forced him to resign from the ANC.

'In the name of the law,' Mandela said, 'I found myself treated as a criminal . . . not because of what I had done, but because of what I stood for, because of my conscience.' His public voice might be silenced but, like most of the banned people, he continued working behind the scenes, illegally lecturing to groups in the townships.

Meanwhile, he had become a devoted family man. He and Evelyn had three children, two boys – Thembekile and Makgatho – and a daughter, Makaziwe. He enjoyed their companionship and longed for them to know the world of his own

Mandela with Oliver Tambo

childhood, but there was now no escaping Johannesburg and Orlando's bleak landscape, which lay under a pall of smoke from the thousands of cooking fires. Had he been white, as a lawyer he would have lived in a large house, most probably with a swimming pool, in a beautiful suburb with trees and gardens.

After qualifying as an attorney, he had set up in partnership with Oliver Tambo, who had switched from teaching to law. The waiting room of their office overflowed with patient queues of people. Under apartheid laws, for Africans to be unemployed was a crime, to be landless could be a crime, and to brew and sell African beer — which helped increase the small family income — was a crime. To cheek a white man could be a crime, and to live in the 'wrong' area was a crime.

Mandela regularly wrote articles about these conditions. He was particularly angered by laws which made it illegal for an African to have his family living with him, and which gave Africans a 'Bantu', inferior, education.

While the government was increasing racial and tribal divisions, the ANC and its Indian, white and Coloured allies were uniting people. In June 1955 they held a Congress of the People which Mandela regarded as a 'spectacular and moving' event. Though he was banned from attending, he had been consulted about the Freedom Charter adopted by the Congress. This began:

> 'We the people of South Africa declare for all our country and the world to know; that South Africa belongs to all who live in it, black and white, and that no government can justly claim authority unless it is based on the will of all the people.'

Later that year Mandela's bans ran out. He was promptly restricted for a further five years. Friends had noticed that the political pressures were undermining his marriage, and eventually he and Evelyn were divorced. After work on Fridays he fetched the three children from their mother's home and they spent the weekend with him.

5 Could This Be High Treason?

At dawn on 5 December 1956 there was a loud knocking on Mandela's front door. 'Maak oop! Open up, police!' All over South Africa scores of men and women of all races were similarly awakened, to be arrested for High Treason. Mandela was taken by armed police to the Fort, Johannesburg's old prison. Sisulu and Tambo were there, and the ANC's great leader, Chief Albert Lutuli, from Natal.

When the trial opened in Johannesburg, vast crowds singing freedom songs filled the streets around the court and the prisoners were driven up in a convoy of *Kwela-kwelas* – police vans. The State alleged that the Freedom Charter was a step towards revolution and that the accused were aiming at a communist society. The defence lawyers roundly rejected these charges, declaring that not only were 156 individuals on trial, 'but the ideas that they and thousands of others in our land have openly expressed.'

In due course, the accused were granted bail and allowed to live at home or, for those from distant parts, to stay with local families. The State case was a muddle – among the thousands of documents solemnly produced in evidence were signs seized from a lunch stall at the Congress of the People! SOUP WITH MEAT and SOUP WITHOUT MEAT.

As the monotonous days passed it was hard for the accused to stay awake for serious moments when the State tried to prove violence in the Defiance Campaign, and insisted that many documents, including Mandela's speeches and writings, were revolutionary.

Mandela and Tambo were among the few who could carry on part-time with their jobs. Most of the others, a long way from their homes, suffered great hardship even though their families were supported by a fund set up by leading churchmen and liberals, with generous support from Christian Action in London.

After more than two years most of the accused had been released. But, in a Pretoria court 30 remained on trial, among them Mandela and Sisulu and a British born social worker, Helen Joseph. For yet another year it dragged on, while throughout the country anti-government protests multiplied. Chief Lutuli appealed to people overseas not to buy South African fruit and not to send arms and oil to a government which savagely repressed its people.

In February 1960, the British Prime Minister, Harold Macmillan, shocked the South African parliament by telling them that a 'wind of change' was sweeping Africa. A few weeks later, on 21 March, at a township called Sharpeville, south of Johannesburg, police fired into a crowd protesting against the pass laws — sixty-nine Africans were killed and nearly two hundred wounded. Most were shot in the back. They included children. That evening, 1,600 kilometres away at a

Mandela and others in the Treason Trial

township outside Cape Town, police shot two Africans dead, and injured forty-nine.

Horror and rage swept the country, setting off riots, strikes and huge protest marches. SHARPEVILLE – the name flashed around the world, setting off a storm of condemnation.

The South African government declared a State of Emergency and banned the ANC. Mandela and the others in the Treason Trial were among thousands imprisoned, cut off from their people and unable to help in this terrible crisis. Oliver Tambo had already left for Britain to set up ANC offices in exile.

It was at this time that Mandela made a great impression on important Britons and Americans who were attending the trial. The defence team withdrew, protesting that a political trial should not be held during a State of Emergency. Mandela took over the defence, with Duma Nokwe, another lawyer, and he was also an excellent witness. In the course of prolonged cross-examination by the State he was asked, 'Isn't your freedom a direct threat to the Europeans?'

'We are not anti-white,' he replied. 'We are against white supremacy and, in struggling against white supremacy, we have the support of some sections of the European population.'

The judge, referring to the ANC's demand for 'one man one vote', asked Mandela what the value was of people who know nothing taking part in elections. Mandela, only just managing to control his anger at the phrase 'people who know nothing', retorted that his own father had had no formal education but had he been given the vote, he would have had the ability and the sense to use it responsibly.

Questioned about communism, he said he had not become a communist, adding that he was impressed by the absence of a colour bar in the Soviet Union and by the fact that it had no colonies in Africa. When it came to international affairs, he pointed out that Africans watched the voting at the United Nations – whereas Russia and India were among those on their side, America often voted with the South African government.

At long last after 4½ years, on 29 March 1961 the

accused stood in the dock, awaiting the judgement. 'You are found not guilty,' said the judge. 'You may go.' Triumphantly they left the court – Mandela an exuberant figure towering over the crowd as they carried their lawyers shoulder high, to be greeted by a cheering, dancing crowd. Outside they all sang *'Nkosi Sikelel' iAfrika'*.

6 How Many Bridesmaids Do You Want?

'Surely you know Winnie from Bizana?' With those words Oliver Tambo introduced Nelson Mandela to Winnie Nomzamo Madikizela, who came from his own birthplace, Bizana in the Pondo area of the Transkei.

A lovely, vivacious young woman in her early twenties, Winnie's picture had appeared in local magazines when she had been appointed the first black medical social worker at Baragwanath, a big African hospital.

Some time later – after the Treason Trial had begun – Mandela invited her to lunch. Overawed by this famous man, she excitedly accepted. It was a Sunday and he broke off from his legal work to take her to a popular Indian restaurant. She had never tasted curry and, choking on the hot spices, nearly wept with embarrassment as he noticed and offered her a glass of water. 'It helps to take a sip,' he urged.

People kept coming up, wanting his advice or a friendly word. To have a chance to talk, he drove Winnie to a patch of countryside where they went for a walk. All she recalls of their conversation was his asking her to help raise money for the Treason Trials Defence Fund. Perhaps it was then that he learned that she shared his love for the landscape of the Transkei, that she too had herded cattle and goats. Her father had been principal of a school and Winnie, after her mother's death, had cared for her younger brother and sisters from the age of nine.

'If you are looking for some kind of romance, you won't find it,' Winnie has said of what followed. Sometimes she watched Nelson 'sweat it out' in the gym. At other times they visited friends in the townships and suburbs. Deeply in love, she yet remained in awe. One day when they were driving along Mandela suddenly stopped the car and asked her to visit a dressmaker who would make her wedding dress. He then asked, 'How many bridesmaids would you like?' Winnie accepted with another question, 'When is the wedding to be?'

Although her father was impressed by his daughter's engagement to so highly respected a man, there were grave anxieties – divorce was frowned on in African society, especially the divorce of a member of the royal family who should set an example. And, even more worrying, Mandela was on trial, accused of treason. But Winnie found that he inspired confidence and courage, and she realized that if you were caught up in the cause, you could no longer think of personal matters. Mandela could not be separated from the people and their struggle for freedom. Only long after did she speak wistfully of the young bride's life which she never knew.

They were married at her home in Pondoland in June 1958. He had been granted four days' leave from

Nelson and Winnie Mandela at their wedding

the order confining him to Johannesburg. This was not long enough for them to go to his home as well – for the double ceremony that was the custom. Ever since, Winnie has kept part of the wedding-cake for the day when her husband emerges from prison and they can complete their traditional vows.

Back in Johannesburg, she made the small house, 8115 Orlando, colourful, and turned the patch of ground allowed to such ghetto houses into a bright garden. Thembi, Kgathi and Maki sometimes came for a weekend.

Within months Winnie was having her first experience of prison. With others protesting against the pass laws being extended to women, she was locked in a cell with only a mat and filthy blankets, and she was pregnant. Mandela was proud of her.

Fragments of family life were all they had together. After his early morning jog, Winnie greeted him with a glass of orange juice. No sooner was breakfast over than he had to drive 64 kilometres to the treason court in Pretoria.

Both their daughters were born during the trial, first Zenani, then Zindziswa. Many years later, from a prison cell, Mandela recalled his wife's patience, the loving remarks which came daily, and the blind eye she turned towards, 'those numerous irritations that would have frustrated another woman.' 'My only consolation,' he added, 'is the knowledge that I then led a life where I'd hardly time even to think.'

Winnie has described how, at the end of the trial, her husband suddenly drove up to the house, accompanied by Sisulu and other ANC leaders. 'They all stood outside in the driveway and he sent a child to call me. On my arrival he simply said, "Darling, just pack some of my clothes in a suitcase with my toiletries. I will be going away for a long time. You're not to worry, my friends here will look after you. They'll give you news of me from time to time. Look after the children well. I know you'll have the strength and courage to do so without me." '

7 The Black Pimpernel

Mandela went 'underground'. At this critical time after the outlawing of the ANC, he was chosen to lead the struggle. Since he would be continually hunted by the police he had to work secretly, sacrificing family life as well as his legal practice. 'No-one in his right senses would choose such a life,' he said later, 'but there comes a time when a man is denied the right to live a normal life, when he can only live the life of an outlaw because the government has so decreed to use the law.' He could not have done so without Winnie's courage to inspire him.

It was difficult for a well-known public figure, especially so striking and tall a man, to disguise himself but, amazingly, he succeeded – wearing a chauffeur's white coat and peaked cap, a municipal policeman's black uniform or a night watchman's long overcoat and woollen hat. His immediate task was to organize a nationwide stay-at-home strike to take place at the end of May 1961. After ten years of confinement to Johannesburg it was wonderful to tour the country. At night he attended small gatherings in the townships, and he moved through cities, meeting factory workers and groups of Indians. Always eager to find points of agreement, he called on white newspaper editors to explain, to listen to their criticisms and arguments, and argue back. While staying with friends in Port Elizabeth, he taught their small sons to box. Back in Johannesburg, late at night, he visited his family.

He had narrow escapes from the police, once having to slide down a rope from a second-floor flat! The press named him the 'Black Pimpernel', adapting the name of the daring character in a novel about the French revolution. Among other organizers working with him

Walter Sisulu

was Walter Sisulu, wise and shrewd, and vital to the planning. They circulated leaflets proclaiming: ARRESTS CANNOT STOP US. VOTES TO ALL. DECENT WAGES FOR ALL. END PASS LAWS. FORWARD TO FREEDOM IN OUR LIFETIME.

The government called up police and military units and hundreds of whites were sworn in as special constables. To frighten people, armoured cars roared through townships by day and, at night, helicopters hovered above the houses, flashing searchlights down. Employers threatened to sack strikers.

Yet, on Monday, 29 May 1961, hundreds of thousands of Africans, and many Indians, risked arrest and loss of jobs and homes to respond to Mandela's call to stay at home. He praised the magnificent response and the hard work from organizers working at great personal risk; but overall there was disappointment, and on the second day he called the strike off. Secretly interviewed by a British television team, he spoke of government violence in face of unarmed, desperate people. 'The question being asked up and down the country is this,' he said gravely. 'Is it politically correct to continue preaching peace and non-violence when dealing with a government whose barbaric practices have brought so much suffering and misery to Africans?'

From underground he circulated a message to his people, 'I shall fight the government side by side with you . . . only through hardship, sacrifice and militant action can freedom be won. The struggle is my life. I will continue fighting for freedom until the end of my days.'

With a small group from the banned ANC and Communist Party he formed *Umkhonto we Sizwe* – Spear of the Nation. It was a hard decision to turn to violence. They chose sabotage – the blowing up of symbols of apartheid, of telegraph lines and other means of communication – and instructed saboteurs on no account to injure or kill people. The problems were immense. The police had a record of most politically active people and, as always in a police state, there were many informers. Telephones were tapped. And there was the possibility of the death penalty.

As the organizing went ahead a small farm was rented for *Umkhonto* in Rivonia, a suburb on the outskirts of Johannesburg. Mandela had a taste of family life when Winnie, Zeni and Zindzi were brought there secretly. He could take the children for walks in the big garden. Three year old Zeni came away with a dream that this was her home. Winnie also brought Thembi, Makgatho and Maki on visits. Thembi, aged twelve, fearing he might never see his father again, asked for a pair of his trousers to wear, as though that would bring him closer.

December 1961 marked an end and a beginning. The ANC's long history of non-violence was honoured as Chief Albert Luthuli was awarded the Nobel Prize for Peace. A few days later *Umkhonto we Sizwe* saboteurs attacked targets in Johannesburg, Port Elizabeth and Durban. One saboteur was killed.

In January, Mandela slipped across the border and flew to East Africa to address an important conference. Reunited with Oliver Tambo, he toured many African states, arranging for assistance for *Umkhonto* as well as scholarships for young ANC members. Briefly in London he met political leaders, and in Algeria took a short military course so that, if necessary, he could fight alongside his people.

It was a thrilling experience. 'Wherever I went,' he said, 'I was treated like a human being.' For the first time he was 'free from the idiocy of apartheid, from police molestation, from humiliation.' He saw black and white people mingling in hotels and cinemas, and using the same buses and trains – impossible in his own country.

He made the perilous return to South Africa. After reporting on his tour to *Umkhonto* groups, he was driving north from Durban when three carloads of police forced him to stop. No-one has said how the police got the tip-off.

So it was that Mandela was captured on 5 August 1962. He had been underground for seventeen months. He was imprisoned in the Johannesburg Fort.

8 'I Will Still Be Moved . . .'

Slogans painted on township walls demanded FREE MANDELA! Overseas there were calls for the release of this 'resistance fighter'. As protests against his imprisonment spread around South Africa, the Minister of Justice banned gatherings which supported him. Yet crowds swarmed outside the court in Pretoria on 22 October 1962. Inside, police and public packed the court. Winnie Mandela, proudly wearing Pondo dress, was there with relatives from the Transkei.

Mandela entered, wearing a jackal-skin robe presented by people in Thembuland. Spectators rose to their feet as he called, '*Amandla*!' – Power. They responded with '*Ngawethu*!' – to the People.

The State charged him with inciting African workers to strike, and with leaving the country without proper travel documents. 'I plead not guilty on both charges,' he declared. The police, who at the time of the stay-at-home had called it a total failure, now gave evidence of its success. The prosecutor pointed out that Mandela had encouraged protest from people for whom it was a crime to strike, such as African mineworkers and servants.

The magistrate, saying he had no doubt that Mandela

was the 'leader, instigator, figurehead, main mouthpiece and brains,' behind the strike, found him guilty on both charges.

In the course of a long statement, Mandela pointed out that for fifty years the ANC had tried to find peaceful solutions to the country's problems, only to be treated with contempt. 'The government set out,' he said, 'not to heed us, not to talk to us, but rather to present us as wild, dangerous revolutionaries, intent on disorder and riot, incapable of being dealt with in any way save by mustering an overwhelming force against us . . . The government behaved in a way no civilized government should dare behave.'

Winnie Mandela and her two daughters

He was confident that the court would not say that his people should say and do nothing. 'Men are not capable of doing nothing, of saying nothing, of not reacting to injustice, of not protesting against oppression, of not striving for the good society and the good life,' he said. Even though it was dreadful for Africans in South Africa's prisons, he and others would continue to protest. 'For to men,' he added, 'freedom in their own land is the pinnacle of their ambitions.' And he expressed a passionate hatred for race discrimination – the way white children were brought up to look down on people with darker skins.

He was sentenced to five years' imprisonment. As he was driven away in a police van the crowd half-marched, half-danced along the street, singing '*Tshotsholoza Mandela*!' – Struggle on Mandela.

Winnie had smiled and waved him on his way. Zeni and Zindzi were too young to understand. Winnie told a journalist, 'All the oldest one knows is that her daddy was taken by the police.' She added, 'I will continue the fight.' Back home she was placed under banning orders.

In Pretoria Central Prison Mandela, wearing prison uniform of baggy shorts and tunic with sandals, was locked in a small cement-floored cell. Felt mat and blankets, sanitary pail, enamel dish and mug, were its furnishings. Woken before dawn by alarm bells and commands shouted in Afrikaans, he followed his usual strict routine of exercises. Twice a day he walked in a yard with other political prisoners. Much of the day was spent sewing mailbags.

9 'Rivonia Is A Name To Remember'

'Accused No.1, Nelson Mandela, do you plead guilty or not guilty?'

'The government should be in the dock, not me,' Mandela declared. 'I plead not guilty.'

Just a year after his imprisonment, he was again on trial, but this time on deadly serious charges, and in Pretoria's Palace of Justice. Alongside him in the dock were Walter Sisulu and seven other men (members of the ANC, of *Umkhonto we Sizwe* and of the Communist Party) – four Africans, an Indian and two whites. Most had been captured at the house in Rivonia.

Distinguished observers from abroad were present for the opening of the State case on 3 December 1963, drawn partly by Mandela's fame and partly by concern at the increasing inhumanity of the South African government's policies. The prosecutor, Dr Percy Yutar, dramatically outlined the State case, alleging not only sabotage but plans for guerrilla warfare, leading to 'confusion, violent insurrection and rebellion' – followed by invasion by foreign armies. He produced one hundred and seventy-three witnesses and stacks of documents the police had found at Rivonia.

The defence team was led by Bram Fischer, QC, an

Afrikaner who had been a communist since studying at Oxford in the 1930's. He told the men that they must prove they had not actually decided on guerrilla war, and also that it was *Umkhonto* policy not to harm human beings. 'I must be frank,' he added, 'even if we succeed, the Judge may yet impose the death sentence.'

'You are concerned with saving our lives,' Mandela said. 'We are also concerned with that, but it's a secondary consideration. Our first concern is the fulfilment of our political beliefs. We have fought for

Demonstrators outside Mandela's trial

freedom and dignity, and what matters is what is politically right. After all, we are only going to tell the truth.'

On Monday, 20 April 1964, in a packed court, Winnie Mandela sat with her mother-in-law who had come up from the Transkei. Dignified and strong despite her age, Mrs Mandela was very proud of her son.

Bram Fischer rose to address the Judge, 'The defence case, My Lord, will commence with a statement from the dock by Accused No.1, who personally took part in the establishment of *Umkhonto we Sizwe*.'

Mandela stood, adjusting the spectacles he wore for reading, and calmly began, 'My Lord, I am the first accused. I hold a Bachelor's degree in Arts and practised as an attorney in Johannesburg for a number of years with Oliver Tambo. At the outset, I want to say that the suggestion made by the state that the struggle in South Africa is under the influence of foreigners or communists is wholly incorrect. I have done whatever I did, both as an individual and as a leader of my people, because of my experience in South Africa and my own proudly felt African background, and not because of what any outsider might have said . . .

'I must deal immediately with the question of violence. Some of the things so far told to the court are true and some are untrue. I do not, however, deny that I planned sabotage. I did not plan it in a spirit of recklessness, nor because I have any love of violence. I planned it as a result of a calm and sober assessment of the political situation that had arisen after many years of tyranny, exploitation and oppression of my people by the whites.'

He spoke for more than four hours. Towards the end he referred to the attitudes of the whites, 'Whites tend to regard Africans as a separate breed. They do not look upon them as people with families of their own; they do not realize that they have emotions – that they fall in love like white people do; that they want to be with their wives and children like white people want to be with theirs; that they want to earn enough money to support their families properly, to feed and clothe them and send them to school. And what "house-boy" or "garden-boy" or labourer can ever hope to do that?'

And he described exactly what Africans wanted. 'Above all,' he concluded, 'we want equal political rights, because without them our disabilities will be permanent. . . . It is not true that the enfranchisement of all will result in racial domination. . . . The ANC has spent half a century fighting against racialism. When it triumphs it will not change that policy . . .' The African struggle, he said, was a struggle for the right to live.

Then he ceased reading. The court was dead-still. He looked up at the Judge and said, 'During my lifetime I have dedicated myself to this struggle . . . I have fought against white domination, and I have fought against black domination. I have cherished the ideal of a democratic and free society in which all persons live together in harmony and with equal opportunities. It is an ideal which I hope to live for and to achieve. But if needs be it is an ideal for which I am prepared to die.'

His statement was published in many countries. The

judge, on 11 June 1964, said he accepted that the men had not agreed on plans for guerrilla warfare, and that they had ordered that care should be taken that no-one was injured or killed. Then he gave judgement, 'Accused No. 1, Nelson Mandela, guilty'. All but one of them were found guilty.

The question remained whether they would be sentenced to hang. Mandela told the lawyers that if the government thought by sentencing him to death the liberation movement would be destroyed, they were wrong. He was prepared to die, and knew his death would be an inspiration to his people in their struggle.

Abroad there was a surge of protest and the United Nations — by 106 votes to South Africa's one — called for the release of the Rivonia men. WE ARE PROUD OF OUR LEADERS . . . NO TEARS: OUR FUTURE IS BRIGHT, declared banners held high by women waiting in a silent crowd outside the Palace of Justice on 12 June. Standing in the dock, Mandela and the others showed no signs of emotion as they heard the Judge announce, 'The sentence in the case of all the accused will be one of life imprisonment.'

Mandela and the other six blacks were flown to Robben Island Maximum Security Prison. Their white comrade joined other white political prisoners held in Pretoria. A senior prison official stated that for political prisoners a life sentence meant exactly that. One newspaper described the case as 'a classic story of the struggle of men for freedom and dignity, with overtones of Grecian tragedy in their failure. Rivonia is a name to remember.'

10 Mandela Taught Me How To Survive

Robben Island: a small rocky outcrop surrounded by turbulent seas some 11 kilometres from Cape Town. It was mid-winter and on days of dense mist a foghorn from the lighthouse echoed mournfully. Mandela and Sisulu and their comrades were among thirty men held in a special section of single cells. A high wall cut them off from blocks housing hundreds of black political prisoners. Abusive white warders ordered them not to talk to each other. Prison garments – shorts and shirts, a thin jersey and jacket – were no protection against the bitter cold. The food was mostly maize with tasteless soup and black coffee.

Day after day, for months that became years, Mandela – prisoner No.466/64 – and his fellows laboured with pick and shovel in a lime quarry. Through summer it was like an oven, in winter damply chill. After limping back to their section ghostly white with limedust, they made straight for the cold showers before dropping exhausted onto mats in their cells. Locked in for the night, as soon as the warders went off duty, the men's voices joined in prayers and in freedom songs.

Every six months they were allowed to write and

Winnie and her daughters on a visit to Mandela

receive one letter of five hundred words, and a visit of half an hour – only family matters could be discussed.

For Winnie, life without her husband was 'utter hell'. As she tried to adjust she kept re-reading his first letter. And when, at last, she could visit him, they were accompanied by warders, only able to see each other dimly through a small window and hear through a telephone controlled by a warder. Any reference to prison conditions or to events in the outside world – and the visit would be ended. They shared what they could of their lives.

Apart from her visits, the limited right to study meant more than any other privilege to Mandela. Not allowed to keep a diary nor to see a newspaper, he was punished when press clippings were found hidden in his cell. Somehow he and the others picked up information, eagerly discussing every scrap. And somehow they always found something to laugh at. One day they were told, 'All those with drivers' licences, stand to one side!' Mandela and several others, thinking they would be driving lorries, stood aside. They were given wheelbarrows to push. They thought it hilarious.

Mandela kept up his routine of physical exercises. Despite the monotony of prison existence, he found that each day was one of developing friendships and shared experiences. A fellow-prisoner, not a member of the ANC, said the government had two aims, to destroy their morale and to get the world to forget them. 'They failed dismally,' he went on, 'because being in the company of Mandela and Sisulu, instead of being weakened, they made you strong. Mandela taught me how to survive. When I was ill, he could have asked anybody else to see to me. He came to me personally. He even cleaned my toilet.'

At home in Orlando, Winnie told the children about the father they could not remember. In 1969 she was herself imprisoned under the 'terrorism' Act. Alone in a small cell, she felt she had company if a fly or an ant appeared. After five days and nights of interrogation her hands and feet were blue and swollen – she had heart trouble – and she appealed for relief. 'For God's sake,' a security policeman taunted, 'leave us some inheritance when you decide to pop it. You can't go with all that information.'

She had endured five months in solitary confinement when, along with twenty-one men and women, she was put on trial. Several of the others had been tortured. State witnesses gave such flimsy evidence that she and her fellow-accused were all found not guilty. Police promptly re-arrested them for further 'interrogation'. Another seven months, and again the court acquitted them. Winnie had spent 491 days in detention. Within weeks she was not only restricted to Orlando township but placed under house arrest – it was a crime for her to leave her home at night and during weekends.

Mandela had waited two years for her visit. She was permitted a half-hour. Now his days were spent in a team collecting seaweed for fertilizer, back-breaking labour on sand washed by the icy waters of the south Atlantic. In the distance ships sailed to and from Cape Town. The men's hunger strikes and stubborn protests, helped by outside pressure, had won various improvements such as hot water for washing and a volley-ball court, but newspapers were still forbidden – as were 'creative' activities such as carpentry.

In time more frequent visits were allowed, and Mandela's daughters, as teenagers, came to meet their father. Zeni could hardly recognize him from pictures she had seen in which he looked 'fat', but what struck her most was how humourous he was. Zindzi, who had been nervous, was comforted by his warmth. Watching him walk away afterwards, she noticed how young and brisk his stride was.

On 16 June 1976 it was a miserably wet, cold day on the Island. Mandela and the others on the sea-weed

Students demonstrating

spun objected to going out but were forced to do so. Returning later, frozen and filthy, they found the hot water had been cut off. They guessed that some important event had angered the warders. Only later did they learn that the children of Soweto, as Winnie Mandela put it, had risen and fought battles on behalf of their elders.

Huge crowds of determined black school children had protested against having to study in the Afrikaans language. Police shot dead several boys and girls. As the crowd retaliated with stones and sticks, more and more people were killed by the police. Blacks stoned two white men to death.

Police and army, equipped for war, poured into the townships and all over South Africa the events were repeated. Police massacres of blacks had marked South Africa's history but nothing so terrible had been known – a modern armed force moving against schoolchildren. Winnie Mandela, as one of the Black Parents Committee helping bereaved families and speaking for the students, was among hundreds detained for five months.

Not long after her release, police were again banging on her door. They drove her, not to prison, but with Zindzi into banishment, dumping them at a small concrete house in a dusty location in Brandfort. This Afrikaner village in the Orange Free State was the most hostile place the state could have chosen for Mandela's family. But Winnie's black neighbours, warned against this 'dangerous communist', soon responded to her warmth. She organized meals and a playground for children, soup for the aged and a clinic. Foreign embassies helped with funds and equipment. As she encouraged families to grow fruit trees and vegetables, colourful patches sprang up in the location. And in the village even one or two whites were charmed by her.

Her every move was spied on by a gloomy sergeant who repeatedly brought her to court, accusing her of breaking one of her bans. Zindzi became seriously depressed after her young friends were harassed for visiting the house. Only after her father had sent the matter to the Supreme Court was her right to have visitors established. To Mandela's delight she had become a writer and her first collection of poetry won a prize of $1,000 in America. The South African government refused to grant her a passport to go to New York to receive it.

Zeni, meanwhile, had married Prince Thumbumuzi Dlamini, son of King Sobhuza of Swaziland. Their three children, together with Thembi, Kgathi and Maki's families, meant that Mandela had a growing collection of grandchildren. Every morning in his cell he performed a small ritual, dusting the photos of his family on his bookcase, always ending with Winnie's.

11 'Release Mandela!'

One night in April 1982 Mandela and Sisulu, with three other Rivonia men, were abruptly transported to Cape Town, then to Pollsmoor Maximum Security Prison, in the valley beyond Table Mountain.

Locked in a dormitory cell, along with a younger man serving a twenty year sentence, they were isolated from the thousands of other prisoners of all races. The food was better than on the Island, and they could now receive a range of newspapers. But they greatly missed the community life in their section on the Island where they had spent much of the day out-of-doors. In Pollsmoor they could only walk in a yard enclosed by high walls. Mandela now knew what Oscar Wilde meant by 'the little patch of blue that prisoners call the sky.'

During 1984 he was suddenly allowed a 'contact' visit from Winnie. For the first time since 1962 husband and wife could hold each other and kiss – in the presence of warders, of course.

Meanwhile, as the oppression increased and protests grew ever angrier, a campaign calling on the government to 'Release Mandela', and unban the ANC, was gathering strength. The South African Council of Churches said that needless suffering and bloodshed could only be avoided if Mandela and other imprisoned and exiled leaders were freed to help reshape society. Many whites – even Afrikaners – supported the call. In exile, Oliver Tambo's years of hard work had born fruit: the ANC was widely recognized and in South Africa Umkhonto sabotage was intensifying. When a countrywide United Democratic Front of all races was founded, the demands for Mandela's release took on fresh force.

The president, P. W. Botha, was unmoved: it was not the government which stood in the way of Mr Mandela's release, he said on 31 January 1985, it was he, himself. All he had to do was to renounce violence.

Mandela's reply to the president was read by Zindzi to a rapturous crowd gathered in a stadium in Soweto on 10 February. Dressed in jeans and UDF yellow teeshirt, she began, 'My father and his comrades wish to make this statement to you, the people, first.'

Mandela expressed surprise at the government condition for his release – 'I am not a violent man,' he declared, and pointed out how ever since 1952 the ANC had asked one Prime Minister after another for a conference at which *all* the people in South Africa could decide on their future. But these requests were always ignored. 'It was only then when all other forms of resistance were no longer open to us that we turned to armed struggle,' he said. He called on Botha to show that he was different to the other Afrikaner leaders, 'Let *him* renounce violence. Let him say that he will dismantle apartheid.' Mandela's message concluded, 'I cannot and will not give any undertaking at a time when I and you, the people, are not free. Your freedom and mine cannot be separated. I will return.'

Throughout South Africa violence was escalating. President Botha talked of reforms – but little was changing. One Minister insisted that apartheid was dead. 'If so,' commented a black newspaper editor, 'urgent funeral arrangements must be made because the body is still around and making a terrible smell.'

A new parliament, allowing representation for Coloured people and Indians but not for Africans, triggered off a storm of protest. Mandela and his companions could only read about what the rest of the world watched on television: police and army invading townships, shooting down people, children as well, as if they were big game; police whipping protesters. And as thousands were detained – students, trade unionists, churchpeople and leaders of local communities – leaderless mobs stoned police and burned 'collaborators' – black policemen, mayors, councillors and suspected informers who represented the white oppressors.

Up and down the country there were massive funerals. 'Our people are being killed just like swatting flies,' said Desmond Tutu, Bishop of Johannesburg. The black, green and gold flag of the outlawed ANC flew above the crowds and covered the coffins – while illegal freedom songs were sung. Again and again, Botha was urged to release Mandela, talk to him – even President Reagan and Mrs Thatcher added their voices. But Botha remained adamant, despite a country in turmoil and a badly damaged economy.

Police continued to harass Winnie Mandela. Her

Victims of riots

house in Brandfort was petrol-bombed and after she had settled back in Orlando, she was arrested, and imprisoned twice. She could live anywhere in the country except in her own home, and except in

Johannesburg. She fought back every inch of the way — a leader in her own right. Each visit to her husband, she said, recharged her batteries, while he wrote to her saying, 'Had it not been for your visits, wonderful letters and your love, I would have fallen apart many years ago.'

All over the world people have been inspired by the Mandelas. Honours are heaped on them. Although walled in, Nelson Mandela has been made a 'citizen' of Glasgow and Rome, of Aberdeen and Olympia. Typical of other honours is the Place Mandela in Grenoble and the Mandela Gardens in Hull, marking celebrations for the anniversary of William Wilberforce, freer of slaves. Meanwhile, in South Africa millions of young people who were born after Mandela vanished into jail, have come to regard him as their heroic leader.

Winnie, speaking of her husband and the other political prisoners with him said, 'Mandela's spirit remains untouched. All those men are just as untouched. Such total dedication. Such total commitment. No soul erosion whatsoever. They are totally liberated. A government in exile.'